BIONICLE®

Swamp of Secrets

by Greg Farshtey

SCHOLASTIC INC.
New York Toronto London Auckland Sydney
Mexico City New Delhi Hong Kong Buenos Aires

For Walter Gibson and Fran Striker,
who "showed the world new ways to dream."

ISBN-13: 978-0-545-05416-4
ISBN-10: 0-545-05416-8

12 11 10 9 8 7 6 5 4 10/0

Printed in the U.S.A.
First printing, July 2008

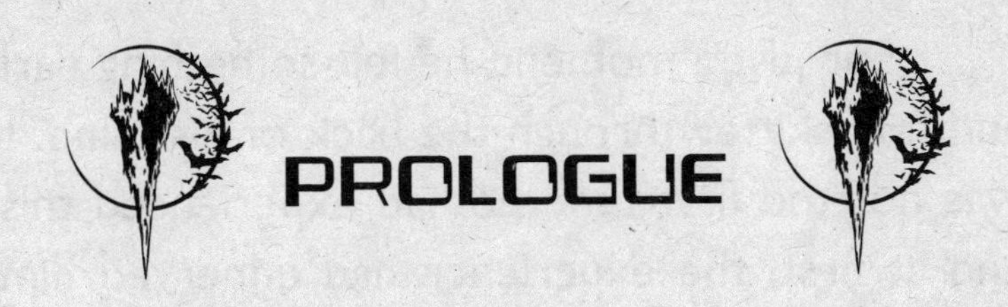

PROLOGUE

Takanuva, Toa of Light, walked along the shoreline of the city of Metru Nui, his keen eyes scanning the waters. He did this every day, waiting for some sign of the Toa Nuva's return.

His time as sole guardian of the city was over. The Toa Mahri had returned, minus one of their number, to help secure Metru Nui. But the Toa Nuva were still missing, and no one knew where they were. He had petitioned Turaga Dume for permission to go searching for them. The Turaga had promised to consider it, but Takanuva was tired of waiting.

I sat here and did nothing while the Toa Nuva almost died on the island of Voya Nui, he thought. *I wasn't there when Jaller and his team risked their lives to save the Great Spirit Mata Nui. Maybe Toa Matoro wouldn't have died if I had been there. Not again — never again!*

For just a moment, he felt something dark and foul skitter through the back of his mind. It was not the first time he had experienced this, and at first, the experience had unnerved him. It was Turaga Onewa who told him that what he was feeling was some other mind trying to intrude on his. Instead of pulling away, Takanuva was supposed to push back to try and find the source.

The Toa of Light steeled himself and thrust with all his mental energy. Suddenly, he saw a picture in his mind. It was only there for an instant, but long enough for him to see that his attacker was in the Metru Nui Archives. Along with the picture came two words, heard as clearly as if someone had spoken them out loud.

Dark Hunter.

Takanuva broke into a run, heading for the Onu-Metru district and the entrance to the Archives. It all made sense now. The band of thieves and killers called Dark Hunters had coveted Metru Nui for thousands of years. They had slipped one of their number into the city, no doubt to stage a sneak attack in preparation for a full-scale invasion.

Good plan, thought Takanuva. *Too bad it's about to turn into such a disaster for them.*

He ran, dashing past Matoran hard at work rebuilding the city, leaping over obstacles, totally focused on his goal. Later, he would realize that if he had been paying more attention to his surroundings, he might have noticed the slime-covered creature that was slithering toward him. He might have saved himself.

Takanuva had almost reached his destination when it struck. The shadow leech leapt at him, attaching itself to his armor with an unbreakable hold. It was hungry, and light was its preferred meal. In the Toa of Light, it had a feast waiting to be eaten.

He screamed as the creature began to drain the light that was his essence. For a normal being, it would have been painful, but for someone who was as bonded to light as Takanuva, it was sheer agony. As the light left him, it was replaced by darkness. Instinctively, he knew that if this creature wasn't stopped, he would be a Toa of Shadow when it was done — if he was still alive at all.

Takanuva stumbled and fell. The pain was getting worse. If he blacked out, it would be all over. He had to do something now.

The leech was clinging to his chest armor, gorging itself on light. The armor had already turned from gold to gray, signaling how close Takanuva was to being lost to darkness. With great effort, he raised his arm and pointed his hand directly at the leech. Then a thin, intense beam of light shot from Takanuva's palm, striking the creature.

At first, it seemed like a terrible mistake. Hitting a creature who fed on light with more light looked to only make it stronger. But with the light came heat — blistering heat. Smoke rose from the shadow leech as it began to burn. When the heat became unbearable, the creature tore itself loose and tried to squirm away. The

Toa increased the power of the beam until the shadow leech was nothing but smoke and ashes.

Then Takanuva collapsed, unconscious. His last thought was whether he would still be a Toa of Light when he awakened, or if it was already too late.

When he could see again, Takanuva looked around in surprise. He would have expected to be in Turaga Dume's chambers in the Coliseum or even in some Matoran shelter in Onu-Metru. Instead, he was in a darkened room that stank of rot. *Am I dead then?* he wondered. *Just waiting for some Po-Matoran to carve my memorial stone?*

"No, you are very much alive."

A figure moved toward Takanuva in the dim light. For reasons he couldn't name, the Toa's first thought was that it was Makuta, come for revenge. But a minor use of his power illuminated the room and revealed the being drawing closer. She was not Makuta, but she was indescribably ancient and disturbingly frail in appearance. Her mask and armor were pitted and scarred from a thousand battles. She looked like a Toa, but her armor and mask design didn't resemble anything Takanuva had ever seen before.

The light revealed another figure as well. This one was also a Toa, though not someone Takanuva recognized. His Mask of Power matched the description of a Suletu, or Mask of Telepathy.

"It is good to see you are still alive," the female said, her voice so soft it could barely be heard. "When Toa Krakua here found you, we thought . . . well, we did not bring you to a place of the dead on a whim."

Takanuva sat up painfully and looked around. He knew what this place was now. He had heard Turaga Whenua describe it. If a Rahi beast in the Archives died, either by accident or in an escape attempt, its body would be brought to this chamber for study. Fortunately, there were no carcasses in the room right now, but it was still a very unpleasant spot to visit.

"Who are you? What's going on?" demanded the Toa of Light.

"I am Helryx, leader of the Order of Mata Nui," came the reply.

"I never heard of it . . . or you."

"If you had, we would have another worry," said Helryx. "As for what is going on, the answer is . . . hopefully not more than your mind is able to comprehend."

"And that Toa?" asked Takanuva. "Is he a member of your little group?"

Helryx shook her head. "Not a member, no. But we needed a courier to bring messages between ourselves and the likes of you, one who could do so without revealing the existence of our Order. So we arranged for a Matoran of Sonics named Krakua to achieve his destiny and become a Toa."

"I must have hit my head when I fell," muttered Takanuva. "Hit it really hard."

Helryx's expression darkened. She held out her hand toward the Toa of Light. Instantly, he found himself pinned to the wall by spikes made of water.

"Fool!" she snapped. "Even now, the Toa Nuva fight for their lives, and only you can help them. But to do so, you must be armed with knowledge . . . the kind only we can provide. So you *will* listen, and you *will* hear!"

It was all a little too much for Takanuva. "Why me? After that attack, I don't even know how much power I have left."

"More than you know," Helryx answered. "In over 100,000 years, the Order has revealed its existence to very few, and then only in a time of great need. This is such a time — and we have need of a unique Toa, one who walks the world of both light and shadow."

"But I'm not —"

"Silence! The time has come to begin."

Helryx gestured to Toa Krakua, who stepped forward. In his hand, he held a small creature. It looked like a cross between the krana who lived inside the Bohrok swarms and the worm-like kraata who dwelled inside Rahkshi armor. The combination was far from pretty.

"Do not fear," said Helryx. "There is much you need to learn and much you need to see. Our little pet is here to provide . . . visual aid."

With that, Krakua placed the creature on Takanuva's mask. A moment later, the world around the Toa of Light fell away. Suddenly, he was seeing events from a time long past, when the universe was new. He heard the voice of Helryx, as if from far away.

"Watch and listen, Toa of Light," she said. "You have much to learn — and time is not your friend."

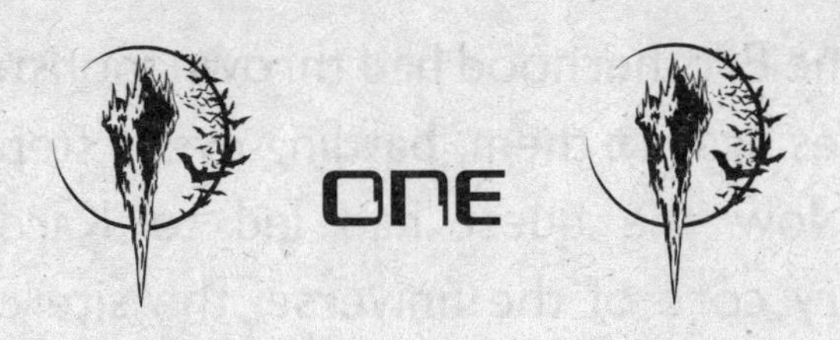

ONE

Tahu Nuva rocketed down toward the Karda Nui swamp. Usually, he would have been planning strategy during the journey, trying to guess what threats might be waiting and how to deal with them. Today, though, just one thought dominated his mind:

It's really a long way down.

He flashed back to just how he and his teammates had gotten here. Over 1,000 years ago, the evil Brotherhood of Makuta had attacked the Great Spirit Mata Nui, plunging that powerful entity into an unending sleep. His absence gave the Makuta the opportunity to seize power in various lands and spread their darkness throughout the universe.

The mission of the Toa Nuva was to rescue Mata Nui from his coma and restore order to the universe. So far, it hadn't been an easy one. The Brotherhood had thrown monsters and menaces against them, battling every step of the way. Now the quest had led to Karda Nui, the very core of the universe, the site of what would be the final battle.

The team had arrived only to discover the Brotherhood was already here. The Makuta had been mounting attacks on the Matoran of Light who lived in this place and were close to succeeding at conquering the region. After a few hard-fought battles, the Toa Nuva realized they had to split up. Half the team stayed above to fight the Makuta, while Tahu, Gali Nuva, and Onua Nuva headed for the swamp.

Now that he thought about it, it wasn't a plan that Tahu was too thrilled about. It went against his nature to run from a fight. But there was good reason to believe that the powerful Mask of Life was at the bottom of the swamp. If the Makuta found it first, they could wipe out every living thing in the blink of an eye.

So here we are, flying through mist so thick even I couldn't burn it away, heading for a mud pool, he said to himself. *Even that wouldn't be so bad, if this place didn't feel so . . . wrong.*

Some time ago, on another island far away, Tahu had visited a site the Matoran called the "place of shadow." It had felt corrupt and unnatural, as if the fabric of the universe was just slightly off. Although he never admitted it at the time, he had found the spot highly disturbing. He had hoped never to experience such a place again, but as he approached the swamp, he knew he had not gotten his wish.

It was hard to see much of anything about the marsh at first, so shrouded was it in mist and fog. As the three Toa Nuva flew closer, they could see clumps of land of varying sizes dotting the murky water, most of them consisting of mud and moss. Thick foliage grew from the bottom of the swamp, but most of the plant life seemed strangely twisted and warped.

The most prominent features were the stalactites which had impaled themselves in the floor of the swamp during what the Matoran called "the Fall." Normally, these sorts of formations would grow from the top of a cavern down, narrowing to sharp points. But having broken off the cave ceiling long before, it was their fragile tips that now served as foundations and their wider ends that were home to Matoran villages far above. Onua Nuva frowned at the sight. He knew enough about stalactites to realize how easily these could collapse under their own weight, sending the villages plummeting into the swamp.

Gali Nuva was paying no attention to that. As Toa of Water, her concern was the mix of liquid protodermis and seawater that made up the swamp. The first thing she noticed was that it was hot, even boiling in some places. Even more surprising was that, despite the heat, it supported life. More than once, she spotted fins or tentacles breaking the slimy surface. She had seen many a creature of the sea in her time, and fought her share, but she was not at all sure she wanted to run into anything that thrived in such a place.

"This place has all the charm of a Makuta lair," she said.

Onua hovered in the air, eyeing the swamp with distaste. "So," he said finally. "Who's up for a swim?"

Gali landed on a patch of mud. Her armored feet immediately sank partway into the mire. "I can't say I look forward to it, but . . ."

"If the Mask of Life is below the surface, what choice do we have?" asked Tahu. "The Makuta would go down there to search for it."

"But would they ever come back up?" asked Onua.

"It may not even be down there," said Gali. "All we know is that it fell here. It could have landed among the vegetation, or sunk in the mud on one of these little islets." She looked around the vast swamp, which stretched for miles in every direction. "It could be . . . anywhere."

"We'll split up and search from the air," Tahu decided. "Pick a direction. If you spot anything, use your elemental power to alert the rest of us. If anything spots you . . . be careful. It's too much to hope the Makuta aren't already here."

* * *

Onua Nuva flew slowly, every sense alert. He had a reputation for being among the wisest of Toa, and his brains told him Tahu was right. The Makuta were somewhere in the swamp, they had to be. They were out to conquer Karda Nui, and the Brotherhood never did things by half-measures. Before they attacked the villages high above, they would want to make sure that the Matoran had no avenue of escape.

Sometimes, having so much knowledge was a curse. Onua knew all too well the history of the Brotherhood and Toa battles with them, thanks to studies he had made on Metru Nui. There had been a few legitimate victories by Toa over individual Makuta, but nothing truly final — the Makuta always managed to vanish into the shadows they loved. Other battles were less clear-cut. He had long suspected that his team's wins over Makuta had somehow been fixed, with the intent of throwing the heroes off the trail of something much bigger.

Perhaps that is what bothers me most, he thought, *the sense that something is not right in all this. The Brotherhood came close to killing the Great Spirit Mata Nui — but why? His death would have meant theirs, too, along with everything else in this universe. Now they concentrate their forces in Karda Nui, yet seem more interested in attacking Matoran villages than anything else.*

On the face of it, it made no sense. If Karda Nui truly was the most important site to someday awakening Mata Nui — and if the Brotherhood wanted to stop that from happening — why not just destroy the place? They had the power. Why leave it intact for the Toa Nuva to find?

Unless . . . they wanted us to find it. Unless they want Mata Nui awakened, even though they know his punishment for what they did would be terrible indeed. Or do they have reason to believe they will escape having to pay for their crimes?

That thought, more than any other, disturbed Onua. As a being tied to the element of earth, he knew how the slightest shift of the soil in one place could lead to a landslide somewhere else. He had learned early on how to manipulate the earth to suit his own purposes. The Makuta had no interest in doing such a thing with earth or water, fire or ice, but they were masters at manipulating others. And if they were somehow pulling the strings now . . . if the Toa Nuva were doing exactly what the Brotherhood wanted done, without realizing it . . .

Then we may not be saving this universe, he realized. *We may be dooming it forever.*

He stopped to rest for a moment on a spit of mud in the center of the swamp. He had seen no trace of the Mask of Life or any Makuta. He had spotted a number of Rahi that would have sent even a Metru Nui archivist running to hide under the bed. The bizarre appearance of the wildlife was puzzling. Why would so many odd specimens be found in the same place?

A loud buzzing made him turn. A Nui-Kopen was darting toward him, on the attack. Onua had seen the large Rahi hornets before on the island of Mata Nui, but never one quite this size. He triggered the power of his

Mask of Strength and swatted at the insect with an armored hand. The blow sent the Nui-Kopen spiraling through the air and into the swamp waters.

Expecting the creature to emerge again right away, Onua braced for another onslaught. Instead, he saw the insect flailing away in the muddy water, wings beating furiously. Then, to the Toa Nuva's shock, the Nui-Kopen started to transform. Tentacles sprouted from its sides, its wingspan expanded, and its tail transformed into a wickedly sharp, barbed stinger. When it flew again, it was as a vastly different creature than it had been just moments before.

It's something in the water, Onua realized, even as he uprooted a tree to use as a weapon. *Some kind of a mutagen that affected the Nui-Kopen — which means the others have to be warned! If any of us end up in the swamp, anything might happen.*

The new Nui-Kopen hovered in the air, waiting for the right moment to attack. Onua

Nuva drew back the tree, ready to swing it when the enemy got close enough. Then something struck the Toa of Earth in the back — just a glancing, painless blow. The next moment, he had dropped the tree and was standing, arms at his sides, rigid.

Onua frantically tried to move. He could feel his organic muscles flexing, but his mechanical parts refused to budge. He was paralyzed.

Someone or something landed in the mud behind him, but Onua couldn't make his head turn to look. A seemingly endless minute went by before the visitor moved into the Toa's line of sight. It was a yellow-armored being with a hideous face and spikes running the length of his legs. He carried a longsword and a launcher of a kind Onua was not familiar with. He looked Onua up and down with narrow, evil eyes and laughed softly.

"I always wanted my own Toa," said the newcomer. "Makuta Bitil's personal 'hero.' Kneel, Toa."

Against his will, Onua Nuva dropped to his

knees. He wanted to ask how this Makuta was controlling his body, but couldn't get his mouth to move.

"It's this," Bitil answered, as if sensing Onua's question. He gestured to the launcher he carried. "A little invention of the Nynrah crafters of Xia. One shot and I control every mechanical part of your body. I could leave you here, on your knees, until you starve . . . or make you wade into the swamp water and drown . . . or even have you kill your friends."

Bitil smiled. "But first I want the others to see what I have done. We will go see Krika. All of us."

As he said that, the mask the Makuta wore briefly flared to life. In the next instant, half a dozen more Bitils appeared, each as undeniably real as the first. Onua found himself forced to rise and jet into the air, surrounded by the duplicate Bitils.

"That's it," said the Makuta. "You know, I always wanted a pet . . ."

* * *

Gali Nuva skimmed low over the water, scanning for any sign of the Mask of Life. It had already been three hours with no trace, and she was beginning to despair of ever finding it. She also found it hard to concentrate on the search when she knew what might be happening to her friends who had remained behind with the Matoran.

It amazed her how a place could look so familiar and so strange at the same time. When they had first arrived in Karda Nui, all the Toa Nuva had suddenly realized they had been here before. It had been ages and ages ago, when they were still so inexperienced. But it hadn't looked like this, far from it. Then again, that had been so long ago.

Not for the first time, she wondered just how many millennia she and her teammates had spent locked in canisters, waiting for the day they might be needed. They had been clear from the start about the importance of their mission. It was their job to someday awaken Mata Nui should the Great Spirit ever succumb to injury or attack. What none of them had realized at the start was that, because their role was so vital, it would be decided they had to be shut away until it came time to play their part.

Would we have agreed, had we known? Maybe. We were still so innocent then, she thought. *But I wonder how much good we might have done in all those years if we had been free to act?*

Gali flew on, wrapped up in her still-fragmented memories. Perhaps if she had been more alert, she might have heard something rising out of the swamp as she passed overhead. Then again, in close to 100,000 years, no one had ever spotted Makuta Gorast until it was much too late.

Tahu Nuva was the first of the team to spot something unusual, although it wasn't the Mask of Life. He wasn't quite sure what it was, though something in the back of his mind told him he should recognize it.

It was a solid sphere with no visible opening, embedded into the stone of one of the fallen stalactites. The structure stood out because it was obviously artificial — made of metal, not rock — and designed by intelligent beings. Tahu doubted it was a Matoran construction, since they spent as little time as possible in the swamp.

If it belongs to the Makuta, it's a threat, he thought. *And if it was created by someone else, it may hold answers. Either way, it's worth checking out.*

Tahu flew toward the sphere, wary of a possible ambush, but still eager to investigate. This was the sort of thing he had hoped for in his first moments as a Toa: exploring the unknown, solving mysteries, and doing it all in the service of justice. His methods might not always have sat well with his teammates, but no one could question his dedication.

He circled the structure, giving it a wide berth. There were no signs of any hostile beings near it, not even any Rahi beasts. There was no visible weaponry either. But Tahu hadn't survived this long by being stupid. He activated his Mask of Shielding, throwing an energy field around himself, then moved in to investigate.

An instant later — impact! Tahu collided with a barrier he could not see. There was a flash of pure power, and the next thing he knew, he was being flung back across the swamp. Stunned, he just barely managed to keep his shield up. It was all that saved him as he crashed into a grove of trees with what would otherwise have been armor-shattering impact.

Tahu tumbled down into the mud and lay there, unconscious. All was still and silent. Swamp birds glanced down from the branches at this strange sight, while insects buzzed around his prone body. Suddenly, the Rahi scattered as the temperature abruptly dropped. A moment later, a pale, white form drifted up through the mud like a ghost. The being hovered for a moment, then turned solid, coming to rest on four long legs lined with jagged claws. Bending low over Tahu, the newcomer prepared to feed.

INTERLUDE ONE

Takanuva's vision of the past . . .

The crimson-armored being opened his eyes and looked around. He did not recognize where he was, nor did he have any idea who the five figures nearby might be. Each of them was lying on a slab, just like him, and each wore colored armor and a mask. But where he was red, they were other hues: white, blue, green, black, and brown.

Of course, it came as no great surprise that he didn't know who these others were. After all, he wasn't sure who he was, either.

He started to rise, then found he could not. Thick metal straps encircled him, keeping him pinned to the slab. Unsure of his identity as he was, he still knew that he did not like being bound. He tried to exert his strength against the bonds, but without success. His frustration and anger grew. And then, suddenly, the metal of the straps was growing soft, turning to molten liquid, running off him and onto the floor.

Did I do that? he wondered, as he sat up.

On the next slab, the white-armored figure had frozen his straps, and then shattered them with the merest gesture. The others had all found unique ways to escape their bonds as well.

"Well, we're all free," said the red-armored being. "Now what? Anyone know where we are . . . or who we are?"

The answer came then, but not from any of them. Rather, it was a voice that seemed to come from every part of the room that spoke in reply. "You are Toa."

The figure in the brown armor jumped down from his slab and onto his feet. "Toa! Hey, that's great. I always wanted to be a Toa." He looked up and addressed his next words to the ceiling. "Just one question: what's a Toa?"

"A Toa is a hero," the voice answered. "Every Toa commands an elemental power, which can be focused through your weapons. Each of you also wears a Great Mask, with a power all its own. You will learn about these powers in time, as well as how to control them."

The white-armored figure frowned. "To whom are we meant to be heroes, and why? You say we have great abilities, but what are we meant to do with them? Too many questions for my taste."

The unseen speaker laughed softly. "You underestimate yourself, Kopaka — yes, that is your name. Questions will always whet your appetite for answers. But now it is time for you to meet."

A lightstone illuminated on the ceiling above Kopaka, as the voice said, "Kopaka, Toa of Ice."

One by one, the lightstones lit above the others as the speaker recited their names.

"Gali, Toa of Water."

"Pohatu, Toa of Stone."

"Onua, Toa of Earth."

"Lewa, Toa of Air."

The last to be named was the crimson-armored figure. "And Tahu, Toa of Fire. He will be your leader."

That seemed to startle Kopaka, who said sharply, "It seems to me we should be allowed to choose our own leader."

"I have to agree," said Gali quietly. "I mean, none of us know anything about this Tahu. What if he's too impulsive to be a good leader? What if he lacks the ability to work with his team members, or can't motivate, or —"

Lewa chuckled. "Or what if he's just a jerk?"

A bolt of flame shot from an irritated Tahu past the Toa of Air, close enough to heat his mask to an uncomfortable temperature. Lewa reached up and yanked the mask off. Immediately, he felt so weak he almost fell over. Pohatu and Onua rushed to support him.

"You must not remove your masks, unless

you are replacing one with another," the voice said. "Without them, your strength is halved."

Lewa gingerly returned the hot mask to his face. "Thanks — *ow!* — for telling us." He turned to glare at Tahu. "And as for you, fireflyer, better be careful a big wind doesn't blow you out one of these days."

"Big wind," Tahu said, nodding. "Yes, that's you, all right."

Kopaka decided to ignore the argument. "So we are a team," he said to their unseen host. "Again, I ask — for what purpose? What are we meant to do?"

A panel slid open in the far wall. Beyond, there was only darkness.

"The gateway to another mystery, perhaps," said Onua. "I wonder if a Toa's life is filled with them."

"Then this will be just the first of many we walk through," Tahu replied. "Let's go."

Beyond the door, there was a long, narrow platform that jutted out into the empty space of a massive, spherical chamber. The cavernous room was totally dark. Only Onua was able to see at all, thanks to excellent night vision the others lacked.

This was not altogether a blessing, because it allowed him to see just how high off the ground they were standing. He peered nervously over the edge of the platform. Being a creature of the earth, heights were not his favorite thing.

There was a sudden burst of light. A symbol illuminated in mid-air and hung silently before the eyes of the Toa. In the center was an oval shape, flanked to the northeast and southwest by two much smaller ones. On either side of the three ovals were larger curved shapes which ended in two sharp points.

The voice spoke again. "Your universe is guided and protected by the Great Spirit Mata Nui. You, in turn, shall be Mata Nui's protectors. What you see before you is the symbol of his might and purpose."

Pohatu was the first to put what all the

Toa were thinking into words. "If he's a 'Great Spirit,' why does he need protection?"

"The universe is vast and holds many dangers," the voice replied. "If Mata Nui should ever be struck down, it will be your role — your destiny — to restore him to power. If that time comes, you will know what to do."

"And in the meantime?" asked Tahu. "Do we just sit around and wait?"

"You will train. You will learn," the voice said. "And, in time, you will go to the aid of the Matoran, who labor to carry out the will of Mata Nui."

"Sure," said Pohatu. "Hey, the Matoran could probably use our help. You know, what with laboring all day to carry out somebody's will and everything."

All five other Toa turned to look at Pohatu. Finally, Gali smiled and said, "All right, Pohatu. Go ahead. Say it."

Pohatu shrugged, looked up, and asked, "Okay, I give up: what's a Matoran?"

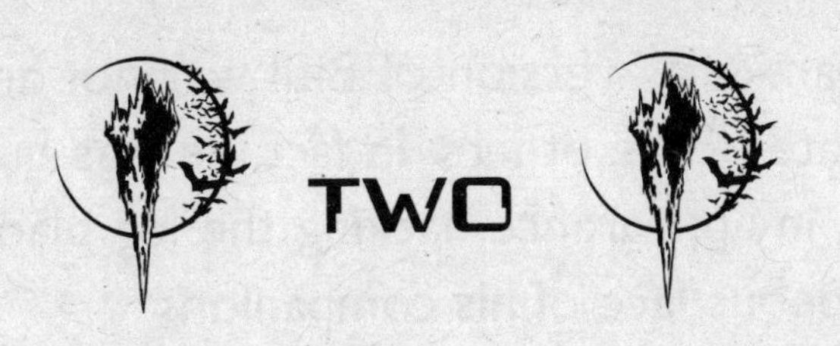

TWO

It took only minutes for Bitil, his doubles, and Onua Nuva to reach Krika's lair deep in the swamp. There was no sign of any living being, only dead Rahi scattered about in the mud. That didn't seem to deter Bitil, who landed on the small islet and stood, waiting.

"Krika? Show yourself."

Onua Nuva wanted to look around to see if anyone was coming . . . and suddenly realized that he could. Whatever Bitil had hit him with had worn off. But he stayed perfectly still, not wanting to let the Makuta know his body was his own again.

"You never see him until the last moment," Bitil muttered. "I hate that."

The other Bitils nodded in agreement, all but one, who looked very confused. Now that Onua took a second look, he realized that particular version of Bitil was not an exact duplicate of the others. In fact, he was quite different in appearance, lacking the leg blades and the hideous face of his companions.

The Toa of Earth had no idea what was going on here. But whatever it was, it had started with the Makuta that had captured him. He waited until that one's back was turned, then charged forward and caught him in a headlock. He swung Bitil around as the others surged forward.

"I wouldn't," said Onua. "Not if you like his head attached to his body."

Six pairs of arms were outstretched toward Onua. Shadow energy began to gather in the palms of twelve hands as Bitil's duplicates prepared to attack.

"What happens to you doubles if the original dies?" Onua continued. "Do you really want to find out?"

The Bitil Onua held prisoner began to laugh. Then, with a mere shrug, he broke the Toa's grip and sent Onua sprawling on the ground in front of the duplicates. "You fool," said Makuta

Bitil. "These aren't just doubles — they *are* me. They are *all* me. Each one plucked from my past to aid me in the present. Instant army, ever loyal, and I can call on as many as I need. See?"

As Onua rose, he saw that six Bitils had become a dozen, then two dozen, then close to 50. Some were standing, some flying, some resembled Bitil exactly and some hardly at all. But they all hated the sight of a Toa.

"Unfortunately, they — *we* — never seem to remember what we see in our own future," Bitil continued. "Shame they won't recall the moment of your death."

Onua had made it to his knees. "Then I guess we better make it . . . memorable," said the Toa of Earth.

Closing his eyes, he called upon his elemental power. Ruled by his will, the substance of the islet exploded, sending tons of mud into the air. Along with it flew Onua, rocketing up and away from Makuta Bitil and his legion.

When he felt he was high enough, he turned to see one mud-spattered enemy flying up after him. Shattered concentration had shut off Bitil's mask power, sending his duplicates back to the past. Onua readied his Midak Skyblaster — and then discovered to his surprise that his weapon was no longer a skyblaster. It had morphed into something resembling Bitil's launcher. *Here goes nothing, then,* thought Onua as he fired.

The rocket hit his foe head on, but the effect was completely unexpected. A sphere of pure energy formed around the Makuta, cutting him off from Onua. The next instant, the sphere dropped like a stone, carrying Bitil all the way back down into the swamp.

Onua banked to the right and flew off. He had to warn the others that the Makuta were here in force . . . if it wasn't already too late. But how to find Gali and Tahu?

Half that problem was suddenly solved. A huge fireball rocketed into the air far to the east. That was a call for help if ever Onua saw one. Angling his wings and triggering the rockets on his armor, he headed for battle.

* * *

Gali Nuva couldn't believe her luck. No, she hadn't spotted the Mask of Life, but she had seen what appeared to be a keystone. The Toa Nuva had discovered some fragments of an ancient tablet in the Matoran villages up above. Inscribed on them were directions for how to awaken the Great Spirit Mata Nui. But the fragments were of no use unless all six of them could be collected and read together.

This particular stone fragment was wrapped up in the vines of a huge swamp plant. She was tempted to jet in and grab it quickly, but memory intruded. She recalled tales the Turaga told of an evil, intelligent plant called Morbuzakh that once tried to crush the city of Metru Nui. There was no telling what the plant life was like down in this strange place. Better to approach with caution.

Makuta Gorast could not believe her luck. Stuck in this miserable swamp, mutated by the waters, and no longer able to shapeshift, she had begun to question her role in the Brotherhood's plan. Surely she was meant for something better than wading through mud, feeding off the small reserves of light in Rahi? Perhaps Makuta Icarax had been right all along . . . this grand Plan involved too much waiting and not enough killing.

She swiftly rejected that notion. The Plan was what mattered, nothing else, and certainly not the needs of any individual Makuta.

But now, Fate had sent her a Toa, no doubt brimming with light. She was tempted to glide in silently on her wing blades and attack, leaving this Toa of Water a corrupted husk in the end. But she had heard tales from other Makuta about how Toa were sometimes the most dangerous when they seemed most vulnerable. Better, she decided, to approach with caution.

A mini-tidal wave of swamp water smashed into the plant, shaking its thick trunk. When the wave subsided, the keystone was still firmly lodged in its tendrils. Gali summoned another fist of water, targeting it right at the spot where the stone was trapped. This time, the fragment actually moved slightly, starting to work its way loose of the plant's grip. Another three attempts, and the stone fell to the soft earth.

Gali went to retrieve it. It wouldn't be long now.

Gorast watched as the Toa of Water harnessed her elemental power to dislodge a piece of rock from a plant. She vaguely recalled Antroz telling her that if she saw such a stone, she should gather it up and deliver it to him. But her hunger for light had driven that order from her mind until now.

Better and better, she thought. *I will drain a Toa and carry out my orders at the same time.*

The keystone was finally loose, and the Toa was headed for it. Gorast dove to attack. It wouldn't be long now.

Gali's fist closed on the stone even as she remembered something else. It was a hazy recollection of something said to her long, long ago. She had been in a barren, unbearably hot place, she recalled. There had been a battle, and she had lost, though not to an enemy. Someone was standing over her.

"The danger isn't always what you see," he was saying. "Often, it's what you don't see until it's too late."

The thought made her turn. Gorast was bearing down on her. Gali didn't bother to think, just reacted, sending a pile driver fist of water slamming into the Makuta.

Gorast spun crazily through the air, finally latching onto a tree with her four clawed hands. Hissing angrily, she rocketed toward Gali. The Toa hurled another water blast. Gorast dodged and plowed headfirst into Gali's midsection. Gali smashed into a tree, tearing it out of the ground and sending it toppling into the swamp.

Gorast landed in the mud and raced toward the fallen Toa. Dazed, Gali still managed to throw a water sphere around Gorast's head, cutting off the Makuta's air. Gorast tried to shake it off, but the sphere held fast.

Gali glanced at her weapon, finding it had

morphed into a virtual duplicate of what Gorast carried. She banished the water sphere even as she fired, sending chains of energy coiling around Gorast like snakes.

"Surrender. Or would you rather go for another swim on dry land, Makuta?" Gali said. "That is what you are, isn't it? Another Makuta?"

"Gorast," said her captive. "Makuta of the Tren Krom peninsula, mistress of the acid falls, conqueror of the Visorak horde — and you are Gali Nuva, Toa of Raindrops."

With a seemingly effortless shrug, Gorast snapped the chains that bound her. "And Makuta do not surrender . . . for the same reasons Toa do not kill."

Gorast fired her Nynrah blaster. Gali dove, narrowly avoiding the shot, and fired quick bursts of water even as she slid through the mud. Gorast batted away the projectiles with her four arms and advanced. Thinking quickly, Gali increased the moisture in the mud beneath Gorast's feet. The Makuta began to sink into the ground, weighed down by her armor. She tried to fly out, but the mud clung to her as if it were alive and hungry.

"You Makuta think we're weak because we don't kill our enemies," Gali said, rising and walking to where Gorast struggled to be free. "But sometimes, killing can be a mercy. Sometimes the worst thing you can do to an enemy is let her live."

Gorast nodded. "And sometimes the worst is to deprive your enemy of that satisfaction." With that said, Gorast shut her eyes and plunged beneath the mud pool. Gali started forward, stunned that the Makuta was committing suicide rather than surrendering. There was no sign of Gorast, not even an air bubble breaching the surface.

"Stupid," muttered Gali. "Didn't life mean anything to her, even her own?"

There was an explosion of mud behind her. Gorast tore out of the ground like an avenging spirit and drove her stinger into Gali's back. "My life doesn't matter," said the Makuta. "Your life doesn't matter. Only the Plan matters."

A huge fireball flew into the sky then, illuminating the horrible sight of a Toa's light being drained away . . . if there was anyone around to see.

Tahu Nuva hated the cold. Perhaps that was why there was always bad blood between him and Kopaka, Toa of Ice. Fire brought warmth and light; it was used to forge masks and tools; it was essential to life itself. Ice brought nothing but death.

Now, as he lay in the mud, he felt a cold that reached into his very muscles and threatened to freeze them solid. He had never felt anything quite like it, not even in mock battle with Kopaka. It didn't feel like physical cold — it was more a chill of the spirit.

Tahu opened his eyes. The first thing he saw was a long, white, vaguely insectoid leg lined with sharp, curved spikes. It shifted slightly in the mud, revealing three more just like it. Whoever they belonged to was bending over Tahu, but the Toa of Fire doubted it would wake him up gently.

Despite the cold, Tahu forced himself to roll away. Once he had put a little distance between him and his vistor, he got the chance to get a good look — and promptly wished he had not. The creature facing him had a long, narrow, white head with bony ridges extending from its brow partway down its spine. Its forelegs were very long, its hind legs shorter, and one arm held a weapon. It looked like some kind of monstrous Rahi and gazed at Tahu with crimson, hate-filled eyes.

"Once, I was like you," the bizarre being said.

"Like me? You mean you were a Toa?" asked Tahu. He was on his feet now, weapon at the ready.

The creature laughed. It sounded like a skeleton being crushed underfoot. "No. Once I was alive like you: solid and whole, needing no one and nothing. I was Makuta Krika, my name whispered in legends throughout half the known universe. And now . . ."

"What changed?" asked Tahu. He had noted how softly this being was speaking, an old trick to draw a potential victim in closer. The Toa had no intention of falling for it.

"Everything changed, Tahu . . . oh, yes, I know who you are," said Krika. "It changed the day Makuta Teridax unveiled his plan to conquer the Great Spirit and we fell into step behind him — some out of fear, some out of greed, some for . . . other reasons."

Krika shrugged, the wickledly sharp ends of his forelegs rising out of the mud for just a moment before sinking back in. "Our great Plan. It has cost the Brotherhood of Makuta much time and treasure. It has cost me far more."

"Why are you telling me all this?" Tahu asked.

"Do you know why the Brotherhood of Makuta hates Toa so much?"

"I could think of lots of reasons," Tahu replied.

"It's because you are what we could only pretend to be, once upon a time: heroes who do good for no reward. You are given freely the honor and acclaim that could never come fast enough for us. And so we call you fools, and worse, and slay you . . . because we cannot be you."

"Am I supposed to feel sorry for you?" snapped Tahu. "After all the evil you and your kind have done? I don't think so. Share your burdens with someone who cares."

Krika shrugged again. "I simply thought that you would want to know . . ."

The temperature suddenly dropped sharply. This time, Tahu felt as if the energy was being drained from his body. Too weak to stand, he fell into the mud.

". . . Why it is you have to die," finished the Makuta.

The world was starting to spin around Tahu. He was going to have time for one action, and if it didn't work, he would be a dead Toa. With enormous effort, he raised one arm and hurled a huge fireball straight and high into the air. He could only hope Gali or Onua would see it in time.

Krika glanced up, his eyes following the flight of the fiery object. He smiled, but it was a sad smile, for he knew Toa all too well. Tahu's flare would bring more running to their deaths. They were doomed.

And perhaps, thought Krika, *that is the one thing I have in common with my foes.*

INTERLUDE TWO

Takanuva's vision of the past continues . . .

Gali hit the ground hard, and not for the first time. By now, her muscles ached, her armor was cracked in a few places, and her Mask of Power had already been knocked off half a dozen times. She was tired, she was irritated, and she still couldn't see the point of any of this.

"I'm a Toa of Water," she grumbled as she got to her feet. "So what am I doing here?"

Her trainer, Hydraxon, shook his head. "You're a Toa of Water. That's true. So naturally your foes will be sure to attack you only when there's plenty of water around . . . that's *false*."

Faster than her eye could follow, he whipped a boomerang at her. It swooped low and struck her in the legs, knocking her off her feet again.

Hydraxon gestured at the landscape around them. It was barren desert for as far as the eye could see. The humidity in the air was close to zero. "If you want water, you're going to have to make it yourself," he said. "Provided I don't carve you up before you get the chance."

Gali sprang up this time and charged Hydraxon, swinging the hooked tools she carried. He caught one on his armored wrist, grabbed her arm with his free hand, and tossed her over his hip. She landed flat on her back.

"I could do this all day," Hydraxon said, smiling. "And if you keep thinking with your heart, not your head, I'll probably have to."

Gali scrambled to her feet, but this time she didn't attack. Instead, she took a few steps backward, keeping her eyes trained on Hydraxon's hands. If he was going to toss another blade or boomerang, this time she would be ready.

As it turned out, his hands never moved. Instead, he lashed out with a kick at a nearby dune, spraying a load of sand into her face. While she was blinded, he threw two knives, knocking both hooks from her hands.

"Now you're disarmed, *and* you can't see," he said. "That means you have about half a second to live, and that's if your enemy's slow."

Just keep talking, Gali thought. *We'll see who has how much time left.*

Concentrating hard, she fired a jet of water from the palm of her hand. It hit Hydraxon with the force of a small explosion, knocking him to the ground. When her vision cleared, she saw him reaching for one of his weapons. She fired again, pinning him to the ground with her water blast.

"Give up?" she asked.

"Not even a little," Hydraxon replied.

Gali heard movement behind her too late. A silver energy hound slammed into her from behind, putting her face-first in the sand. With her concentration shattered, her water blast was cut off. Hydraxon got up, grabbed her by the back of the neck, and hauled her to her feet.

"Meet Spinax," he said, gesturing to the four-legged beast who still eyed her warily. "After I'm done training you would-be heroes, I have a new assignment, and he's coming along. For now, though, he helps me prove a point — the danger isn't always what you see. Often, it's what you don't see until it's too late."

Gali spat out sand. Somehow, she managed a smile. "I don't envy the group working with you in your next job."

To her surprise, Hydraxon's face darkened. "You shouldn't. Trust me, you shouldn't envy them at all."

Suddenly uncomfortable, Gali tried to change the subject. "So, lesson learned. Are we done for today?"

Hydraxon, who had been lost in thought, suddenly seemed to remember she was there. "Hmmm? No, no. You have a 15-minute head start. Then I send Spinax after you. They say he can track a wisp of energy across a planet and back . . . so I suggest you start running."

"And what am I supposed to learn from that?" demanded Gali.

"It's not training for you," replied Hydraxon, smiling. "It's training for him."

By the time Gali made it back to the Toa's shelter, she was exhausted and sore. "Mask of Water Breathing," she sighed. "Big help when there's no water anywhere around."

Pohatu laughed. "I thought I'd be able to outrun the little beast with my mask, but darn thing never gives up. Ran so fast I fused some of the sand to glass, and Spinax still caught me the second I slowed down. Kopaka's the only one who passed that test."

Gali turned to the Toa of Ice. "What did you do?"

Kopaka shrugged. "I froze him."

"You didn't!"

"He did," said Lewa. The Toa of Air was floating halfway off the floor. Determined to master his Mask of Levitation, his feet were almost never on the ground anymore.

"So what happened?" asked Gali.

"Nothing," muttered Kopaka.

"Nothing?" Onua chuckled. "Hydraxon commended him on his original thinking."

"And then knocked him flat," Tahu added. "Was it six times or eight times in a row, brother?"

"I didn't see you do any better, Toa of Ashes," bristled Kopaka.

"I guess a Mask of Shielding doesn't help much when the boomerangs keep hitting you from behind, huh, Tahu?" said Lewa.

Onua glanced at Tahu and Kopaka and saw neither one was laughing. "Well, we all need to do better," said the Toa of Earth. "Someday, it won't be a trainer we'll be up against, but the real thing."

"That cannot be soon enough for me," said Kopaka. "Perhaps then there will be less talking."

Lewa drifted back down to the ground,

landing beside Gali. "Friendly sort, isn't he?" he whispered.

"He's a loner, but one who's smart enough to know he can't succeed alone," Gali replied. "It makes him angry, but he tries to keep it all frozen inside."

"While Tahu keeps fanning the flames between them, like he's trying to prove something," said Lewa. "Maybe we better stick together, sister. Those two could get us killed."

THREE

In her time, Gorast had taken some pretty hard blows. Some brute named Krekka once tried to stop her from going where she wanted to and made his case with a solid shot that sent her through a wall. (He paid for that, in full, not too long after.) Then there was the time she had been on the wrong end of a Tahtorak charge.

But nothing before could equal Onua Nuva seizing her, lifting her high into the air, and slamming her down with every bit of force his own power and the Mask of Strength could afford him. Even for the raw might of a Makuta, the world spun.

"Stay down while I check on Gali," Onua said, his tone that of an earthquake about to erupt. "And if she's hurt, so help me, I will send you back where you came from in pieces."

Onua took a few steps back so he could

keep an eye on Gorast while looking to his fallen friend. Gali was still breathing and didn't seem badly hurt, only dazed. Whatever this thing was — another Makuta or some form of Rahi beast — and whatever it had been doing when Onua arrived, it evidently had not gone too far.

Gorast hadn't moved, just lay in the mud eyeing Onua with . . . rage? No, the Toa realized, it was something else. Something far more disturbing: hunger.

Onua got Gali to her feet. Gorast scrambled to hers at the same time. "Be careful," whispered Gali. "She's dangerous."

"You are Onua, aren't you? The wise one?" hissed Gorast. "Brilliant and strong, yet never the leader — always forced to follow the orders of fools like Tahu. The Brotherhood would make you a king. You would have all of Metru Nui to rule, Toa . . . all you have to do is stand by my side."

"My armor's black," Onua replied. "That doesn't mean my heart is as well. The answer is no."

Gorast surged forward. Onua met her with a geyser of mud summoned from the ground. As she fought her way through that, he scooped Gali up in his arms and flew, heading toward where the fireball had been. He had to find Tahu so the three of them could stand together.

Gorast took off after him. She knew full well where he was going and wasn't worried at all. The light of three Toa would be a feast to long remember.

Tahu's mind raced even as his body's energy faded away. He had managed to figure out what was happening to him. Krika drained energy from his victims. If there was no one nearby, he took it from the environment. That explained the temperature drops that accompanied his appearances. Now Tahu just needed to figure out a way to stop him.

Temperature . . . heat . . . cold . . . that's the key, he thought. *Wherever he goes, the air turns cold . . . if that's what he's used to . . . maybe I should serve up a little baked Makuta.*

Flame was beyond his abilities just then, but Tahu could still generate heat. He poured what remained of his energy into the ground, willing the soil and water to grow searingly hot until the mud was boiling. Krika gave out a cry of pain and then turned intangible. He drifted above the seething cauldron that a moment before had been just a mere spot of soft ground in a vast swamp.

Tahu didn't care that Krika had escaped. All that mattered to him was that the drain on his energy had stopped. Maybe it was the burns, maybe it was changing to his ghostly form, but Krika's mealtime was over.

The Toa of Fire glanced up and saw more good news. Onua and Gali were on their way. True, they had two vicious-looking creatures on their tails, but the sight of his two teammates was still the best thing he had ever seen.

Tahu absorbed the heat of the ground back into himself long enough for Onua and Gali to land. Krika floated above the three of them while Onua's pursuers circled like Nui-Rama wasps. Tahu forced himself to rise and used his mask power to throw a shield around the three Toa Nuva.

"I see you brought company," he said to Onua.

"It couldn't be helped. Gali has been weakened, and you don't look too well yourself."

"My shield will take a few blasts, and then . . ." Tahu replied. His eyes were suddenly drawn to something in the sky. "Wait, what's that?"

Onua turned to look and noted that all three Makuta were doing the same. What they had spotted was another Makuta, Chirox, plummeting from the sky. He obviously wasn't in control of his flight. Onua guessed he had been on the receiving end of a solid blow from one of the three Toa Nuva battling in the skies above.

Gorast, Bitil, and Krika reacted immediately, flying or floating to intercept their brother. It seemed the perfect time to make an escape, although with Tahu and Gali both low on energy, Onua wasn't sure how far they would get.

"This way," said a small voice off to the left. "Come this way, now."

Onua saw that the voice came from an Av-Matoran. The figure was beckoning to the Toa through some swamp foliage. "I can take you to safety," the Matoran said.

The Toa Nuva of Earth knew it might be a trap, but at this point, he had to take a chance. Tahu nodded his assent, and the three heroes followed the Matoran deeper into the swamp.

They ended up in a small clearing surrounded by lightvines, the plants the Matoran of Karda Nui used as protection against the Makuta. Natural light producers, the vines were painful for the masters of shadow to come near. But what struck the three Toa was what lay on the ground — the bodies of at least a dozen Matoran, all apparently in the midst of some strange transformation.

Onua started to rush toward the fallen villagers, but the Matoran who had guided them there blocked him. "Don't interfere. It's their time, just as it will soon be mine."

"Their time? For what?" said Gali, pushing past Onua and the Matoran. She rushed to the nearest villager. What she saw made her gasp and take a step back.

The Av-Matoran's body was changing before her eyes. Muscle tissue and lung tissue were dissolving, being replaced by metallic protodermis. The shape of the body was changing too, becoming bigger and broader, even as the normal features of a Matoran rapidly disappeared. But that wasn't what shocked Gali and the other Toa Nuva. No, it was that they recognized all too well what the Av-Matoran were transforming into.

"Bohrok," whispered the Toa of Water, shaken to her core. "By the Great Beings, they are turning into Bohrok!"

Krika was the first to notice that the Toa Nuva were gone. Bitil and Gorast wanted to immediately pursue, but Krika waved them off. "Where can they run to? You know as well as I that they cannot leave the swamp without this," he said, raising his foreleg to reveal a keystone embedded between his spikes. With a casual movement, he tossed the stone to Bitil.

"What if they don't find the other five?" asked Gorast.

"They will," answered Krika. "They will because it's difficult, dangerous, and perhaps impossible to do . . . and because they are Toa."

"Be careful, brother," said Bitil. "You are starting to sound like you admire them."

"I respect them and their power," corrected Krika. "You would do well to do the same. We have swept down like a plague and exterminated Toa wherever we found them. Those who have survived have learned to turn any mistake by a foe into a chance for victory."

"Then be careful," said Gorast, leaning in close and locking her gaze on Krika. "Be *very* careful that you make no mistakes, brother — not now, not when a universe is almost in our grasp."

Krika triggered his mask power. The Kanohi Crast, or Mask of Repulsion, sent Gorast hurtling away from him at high speed. She smashed into a nearby stalactite with a sickening thud and hit the mud, dazed.

"I am always careful," said Krika. "And that is how I have survived."

Bohrok. It was a word the Toa Nuva had heard all too often over the last year, and one they had hoped not to have to hear again.

Shortly after their arrival on the besieged island of Mata Nui, the Toa had been faced with a swarm of the insectoid mechanical beings. The Bohrok cut a path of destruction across the island, annihilating forests, mountains, rivers, and anything else that was in their path. It took a desperate effort by Tahu and his team to slow them down and eventually defeat the queens of the swarm. Only recently had the Toa discovered that the Bohrok did serve a benevolent purpose, and the heroes themselves ended up making it possible for them to be unleashed again. Just why the island of Mata Nui needed to be "cleansed" of so many of its natural wonders, the Toa still did not know.

Now, here they stood, watching what had once been a dozen Matoran of Light rise from the earth as new Bohrok. They lacked krana, the small creatures that provided direction for the mechanoids, but in other respects, they looked like every other Bohrok the Toa had ever encountered.

"This is insane," said Gali, horrified. "It can't be true . . . were all the Bohrok we fought once Matoran?"

"Maybe it's not so farfetched," answered Onua. "I remember reading a theory in the Metru Nui Archives that the Bohrok had once been bio-mechanical life and evolved into fully mechanical, artificial life. Isn't that what we just saw happen?"

"It is the way of things," said their Matoran companion. "As the first Bohrok sprang from the first Av-Matoran, so shall the next generation spring from among us. As Bohrok, we serve the will of Mata Nui just as you do. From being merely beings you must protect and look after, we become truly your brothers."

"Of course," muttered Tahu. "When we attacked the queens of the swarm, remember . . . they asked how we could dare to oppose our 'brothers.' We never suspected . . ."

Before Gali's still startled eyes, the twelve Bohrok faded away. "Where have they gone?"

"To join the others and be fitted with the krana that will guide them the rest of their lives," the Matoran replied. "They now have a new role to play . . . as do you. And yours requires this."

The Matoran dug into a pouch he carried and produced a keystone. He handed it to Tahu. "You will need all six to enter the Codrex. Once there, you will know what needs to be done."

"Codrex?"

The Matoran gestured back the way they had come, toward the strange spherical structure Tahu had discovered. "The place of your beginning . . . and your probable ending."

Tahu wanted to ask him more questions, but the Av-Matoran had begun to transform. In a matter of moments, the intelligent being before him had become a mechanized Bohrok. Then it was gone, transported by some unknown means to one of the many nests beneath the island of Mata Nui. And it wasn't the bizarre sight of this change, or even the revelation of the Matoran–Bohrok connection that left Tahu feeling strangely empty — it was the realization that he had never thought to ask the Matoran his name.

And now, he no longer has one, thought the Toa of Fire grimly. *Another sacrifice in the name of the Great Spirit . . . and why? Does Mata Nui have so grand a purpose in life that it warrants so much loss? Or are we all so small in his eyes that he doesn't even notice when one of us is gone?*

Dark thoughts for a dark place, he decided. Tahu sensed a vague memory, buzzing around in the back of his mind like a fireflyer. Someone was speaking to him, a very long time ago, and saying something that would prove to be all too true: "This universe, like all others, demands a price from its heroes."

Tahu understood what that meant. But as he looked around at the now empty swampland, he wondered again why the price had to be quite so high for quite so many.

INTERLUDE THREE

Takanuva's vision of the past continues . . .

Toa Lewa, master of air, rider on the wind, emerald-armored hero in the making, had just discovered something very important. He really, truly, *deeply* hated the water.

Hydraxon's exercise for the day had to do with searching for masks. Someday, he explained, the Toa might find themselves in a situation where Kanohi masks were not easy to come by, and they might have to seek them out. To prove his point, he took all of the Toa's masks and hid them in various places. Each Toa was given a map carved into a stone tablet that detailed where his or her mask could be found.

As the mysterious voice had warned them, without a mask their powers were halved. Lewa found himself wishing it had also warned them about insane trainers, unfriendly teammates, and how water was so very . . . wet.

He took a deep breath and plunged into the ocean again. His Mask of Levitation was supposed to be down here somewhere, but it was so dark he couldn't see. *What I could really use is a Mask of Light right about now,* he said to himself. *Right, like that's ever going to happen.*

Lewa swam further down, disturbing a school of rainbow-colored fish. They looked to him like most fish — placid, slow-moving, with dumb expressions on their faces. At least, that was how they looked until they closed in around him, darting and diving, and biting him with needle-like teeth.

At first, Lewa just found this annoying. Then, the fish started finding chinks in his armor, and their attacks began to hurt. Angry, Lewa tried to summon an underwater cyclone to blow them away. But without his mask, he couldn't generate a force of sufficient power to scatter them.

His lungs were starting to ache for fresh air, and the school of fish wasn't letting up. Lewa kicked his legs and shot to the surface. He climbed back onto the beach and sat down in the sand, staring at the water as if it was his worst enemy.

"Giving up?" asked Hydraxon. Lewa turned to see the trainer sitting on a rock, twirling a dagger.

"No," answered the Toa of Air. "Just . . . frustrated."

"Then you and Gali should get along just fine," Hydraxon said, gesturing over his shoulder.

Lewa rose and looked past the trainer into the woods. There was Gali, standing at the bottom of the tallest tree he had ever seen. Her Mask of Water Breathing was wedged among some branches way at the top. Scars in the tree showed where she had tried to use her hooks to climb it, but the trunk was covered in an oily substance that made it almost impossible to scale.

"Looks like she has a problem," said Lewa. "Bet I'll get to my mask before she does."

Hydraxon sprang from his perch and executed a perfect, sweeping kick, knocking Lewa to the ground. "It's not a race!" he said sharply. "You 'heroes' are incredible. Kopaka has spent all day staring into an active volcano, trying to figure out how he can freeze his way to his mask. Tahu has been melting and re-melting the same iceberg all day, trying to free his. And the other two are no better."

Lewa got back to his feet and glared at Hydraxon. "You gave us these stupid tasks. Each of us is just trying to get ours done. It's not so easy to do when you're on your —"

The Toa of Air abruptly stopped, as he realized what he was saying. Hydraxon smiled and began a slow, sarcastic round of applause. "A light dawns," said the trainer. "I didn't realize it would take light years. Think about the missions I gave the six of you — and tell me when I said you *couldn't* work together?"

Lewa looked down at the sand, feeling a mixture of anger (mostly at himself) and a little embarrassment. It was true, Hydraxon had never insisted they pursue their masks alone. They had just split up as soon as he handed out the maps. Lewa had never even considered working with anyone else, and he doubted any of the others had either.

Hydraxon tossed his dagger from hand to hand. "It's a great weapon — sharp, perfectly balanced, accurate. But it takes more than talent and practice to use it correctly . . . it takes the brains to throw it at the right target. You Toa have plenty of power, but I'm not seeing much in the way of common sense. Without it, all that power isn't worth a pile of protodites."

Lewa looked again at Gali, who had summoned a small rainstorm to try to wash the mask out of the high branches. "Looks like I am going to get wet again," he muttered, already moving to help her.

Gali was surprised when she saw the Toa of Air approaching. She was surprised even more so when he used his weakened elemental powers to add some wind to her rain. The tree began to sway back and forth, until finally the Mask of Water Breathing came loose and fell right into her hands.

"Um . . . thanks," she said. "But wasn't that against the rules of the game?"

"No," said Lewa. "Turns out trying to go it alone is playing the wrong game completely." He looked away, still feeling a little uncomfortable about what he was going to ask. "Well, uh, so . . . can you give me a hand now?"

Even with all their differences, Tahu and Kopaka had discovered one thing they agreed upon: They couldn't stand each other. Despite that, the night after the mask-searching exercise found them hiking through the mountains together.

"There's an easier way to go about this," Tahu said. "Find Hydraxon and make him take us where we need to go. If the door is barred against us, I bet he would make a great key."

"Are all fire types like you? Or are you just uniquely an idiot?" growled Kopaka. "We don't know the extent of Hydraxon's powers. We don't know he wouldn't be able to warn our 'hosts' somehow. We don't even know that we could defeat him."

Tahu's sword went from red-hot to white-hot in an instant, then cooled down again. "Speak for yourself, frosty."

"Excellent. Fine," Kopaka snapped. "What was I thinking? Of course the answer to every problem is violence and destruction. Who needs conversation when you can have carnage?"

Their argument was cut off by the sight of an imposing fortress in the distance. The place bristled with weaponry and was ringed by armed guards. An army of Toa might have been able to conquer it, but two would just be a moment's distraction for its defenders.

"Think they'll let us in if we ask nicely?" asked Tahu.

"I don't know. Think you can fight your way through all of them?"

Tahu shook his head, laughing. "You're not

the only one who can come up with a strategy, Toa of Snow. Now get your hands up."

Kopaka looked at his companion, puzzled. Tahu had already raised his hands, his sword giving off just enough of a glow that both Toa would be visible to the guards. Suddenly, it made sense. As he lifted his hands in the air and resumed marching toward the fortress, even Kopaka had a hard time suppressing a smile.

The fortress guards did exactly what Tahu had hoped they would do. They brought the Toa they had "captured" inside and right to their leader. If Tahu expected the ruler of this land to be some massive, heavily-armored warrior who could snap a Toa in two with no effort, he was to be disappointed. The figure that awaited them *was* a Toa, although one whose armor looked quite different from theirs. Even more surprising, that armor was blue — like Gali, she was a Toa of Water. She looked up from what she was tinkering with, a small vehicle with multiple legs.

"Like it?" she asked. "I am thinking of calling it a 'swamp strider.' Who knows, there might be some use for it someday."

Tahu's surprise was doubled now that it was clear the mysterious voice that had awakened them belonged to her. Kopaka seemed to take the revelation in stride, though, saying, "Who are you?"

"My name is Helryx," the female Toa replied. "I was the first of our kind. It might interest you to know that I saw you created, Kopaka, all of you."

"We want some answers," Tahu interrupted. "We feel we're entitled to them."

Helryx smiled. "Then answers you shall have, Toa of Fire. All that you want . . . and perhaps more than you can stand."

The Toa of Water put down her tools and approached Tahu and Kopaka. She looked from one to the other and then nodded, as if giving her approval. "Brave. Daring. Strong. You and your team are ready to become true heroes. But . . . this universe, like all others, demands a price from its heroes. Sometimes, they have to suffer; sometimes, they have to die. That is the price for living a life that matters . . . for having the power to change, to protect, to *act*."

Helryx gestured for the Toa to follow her. "Come, my brothers. It's time for you to learn what price will be asked of you."

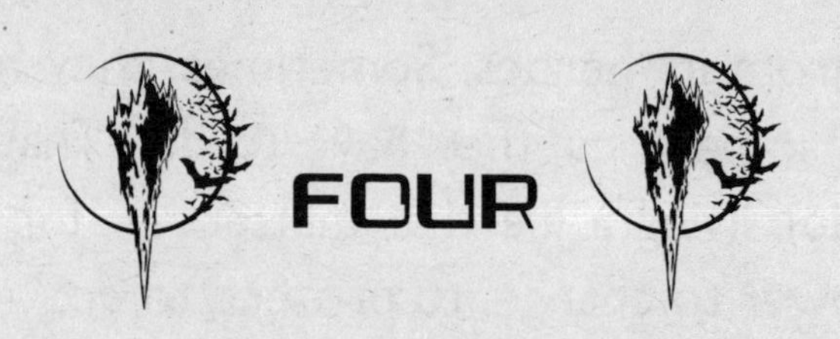

FOUR

Tahu, Gali, and Onua picked their way carefully through the swamp. The Makuta had left a trail a blind Archives mole could have followed. It was obviously a trap, but the Toa Nuva had no choice but to walk into it. They had still found no sign of the Mask of Life, and there was always the chance the Makuta already had it or knew where it was.

"What's the plan when we find them?" Gali whispered.

"Do you remember the one we used when we cleaned out that Nui-Jaga nest on Mata Nui?" Tahu replied.

Gali paused, trying to recall. Then she said, "Wait a second, we didn't have a plan then. You and Kopaka were having one of your arguments. You hurled a fireball, missed, and set the brush on fire. The smoke drove the Nui-Jaga out, and we had to fight them all."

"That's the plan," said Tahu.

"Then it's too bad Kopaka isn't here," Onua said. "You two haven't butted masks in days."

"Onua, you're not helping," said Gali. Turning back to the Toa of Fire, she said, "Tahu, please tell me we actually have some idea of how we are going to deal with three Makuta."

Tahu stopped walking and looked at Gali with a smile. "Watch this — little trick I learned from Pohatu." He looked away from her, concentrating on a spot in the empty air. After a moment, he relaxed again.

"Um . . . nothing happened," Gali pointed out.

"Wait for it," said Tahu.

An instant later, a small ball of fire appeared in midair, right in the spot Tahu had been looking at. It shot down to the ground, starting a miniscule fire. Onua helpfully stamped it out.

"Pohatu and Onua would be best at it,

but we all can do it," said Tahu. "At least, I think so."

"Do what?" asked Gali, growing exasperated.

"Let me try to explain," Tahu said, keeping his voice low. "As a Toa of Fire, I control flame . . . I also control heat, without which you can't have any flame. If I start the process of combustion in a spot, I can time when it actually happens. Then, once it does, I can make the resulting fireball go where I need it to go the same way I would any flame."

Gali looked down at the still-smoldering patch of earth. "So you're saying you can plan a fireball for later?"

"Exactly, the same way Pohatu can set a stone to crumbling inside without it actually collapsing until later. Maybe it's a Nuva ability, I don't know. But I do know we can use this to our advantage — and here's how we're going to do it."

Following Onua's directions, the three Toa approached Krika's haven, taking care to keep as quiet as possible. As Tahu had hoped, all three Makuta were there. Better still, they seemed to be hiding some artifact in a hastily dug pit. The Toa Nuva hoped that might be the Mask of Life.

"Spread out, and be careful," Tahu whispered. "We think with our heads, not our fists, and we'll get what we came for."

Gali tried unsuccessfully to hide a smile. This was a far cry from the Tahu who used to charge into Bohrok nests at the drop of a mask. *I guess we've all grown up in the last year,* she thought.

The three Toa scattered. Tahu took a position to the north of Krika's camp, Onua to the east, Gali to the west. As soon as they were in position, they each put their elemental power to work. Tahu started the process of crafting a huge fireball, Gali a high-pressure jet of water, and Onua a violent quake.

Tahu's creation appeared first, and he used his control over fire to send it hurtling into the Makuta settlement. As soon as it was on its way,

Tahu was on the move. He glanced back to see Gorast coming to investigate.

Next came Gali's water stream, which she was able to steer right into Bitil. Furious, the Makuta charged out of the camp looking for the source of the attack, but Gali was already gone.

That left Krika alone and wary. But nothing he could do could guard him against the earthquake Onua unleashed. Once he recovered his balance, Krika used his mask to repel the ground itself, sending him into the air to search for the Toa Nuva of Earth.

It would take the Makuta only seconds to realize their attackers were nowhere to be found. But that was time enough for Tahu, Gali, and Onua to have circled around and entered the camp from behind. Onua dug up the pit while Gali and Tahu searched the rest of the area.

"Nothing," Gali reported. "No mask."

"Or here," said Tahu, disappointed.

"I've got something," Onua said. "It's not a mask, but potentially useful nonetheless."

The Toa of Fire and Water turned to see that Onua held in his hand a keystone. That made three they had found. If the other Toa had been as fortunate, they had all six. It was a small victory, even if the Kanohi Ignika continued to elude them.

"We had better get out of here," said Tahu. "The Makuta won't be fooled for long."

"Or at all," said Krika. He was standing on the edge of the camp, flanked by Gorast and Bitil. All three looked amused. "Did you really believe we would fall for that transparent ruse? We simply wanted you in one place so we could take care of all three of you at once."

The Makuta fired their ghost blasters as one, but Tahu was too fast for them. His mask power threw a shield up around himself and his team, deflecting the Makuta's attack.

"It's no good, you know," said Krika. "How long can you maintain that shield? An hour? A day? And when it falls, we will take control of your bodies and make you battle each other for our entertainment. Who knows, if one of you survives, maybe we will permit him or her to serve as a permanent slave of the Brotherhood."

"I say we batter the shield down now," snarled Gorast, "and kill them where they stand."

Krika chuckled. "Please excuse my sister — she has always been lightthirsty, even before the swamp changed her. She has a point, though. Time spent here is time wasted in our search for the Mask of Life."

Tahu flashed a grim smile. Even in their desperate situation, it was good to know the Makuta hadn't gotten their claws on the mask yet. With a little luck, maybe they never would.

"You're too late," the Toa of Fire said, trying his best to sound confident. "We already have the mask. It's with Pohatu and the others. They're using it to destroy your brothers even now."

"Ridiculous!" snapped Bitil. "An obvious trick, one I can expose with ease." He concentrated, sending a telepathic flash up to one of the Makuta who lurked in the skies far above. But the message he received back was obviously not what he had been expecting.

"Speak, Bitil," said Krika, impatiently. "How stands the Brotherhood?"

"The Mask of Life . . ." Bitil said, stunned. "It's there . . . it's become a Toa warrior . . . and Icarax has already fallen before its power."

Tahu glanced at Gali and Onua. Both looked just as surprised as the three Makuta. The Mask of Life was a Toa now? It was fighting? What was going on here?

"Time for us to go," Tahu mouthed, no sound escaping his lips.

Gali nodded. She triggered her elemental power, adding more and more moisture to the air in the immediate area until a dense fog began to form. As soon as they were hidden from view, Onua rapidly dug a tunnel in the soft earth. The three Toa vanished into it and were gone by the time the fog dispersed.

"They've escaped!" yelled Gorast. "We must pursue!"

Krika sighed. "Of course we must. We

don't want this to be too easy for them now, do we? Bitil, stop worrying about Icarax — he was a miserable heap of Zivon spittle and no great loss."

Bitil nodded and activated his mask power, plucking three past versions of himself out of the timeline. "Do we follow them?"

Krika shook his head. "Teridax told me once about a remarkable machine the Matoran of his region made called a Keerakh. From his tale, I learned that it is not necessary to chase your quarry — simply be waiting at their destination."

With that said, Krika used his mask to repel the ground and launch into the air. He was followed by the four Bitils and Gorast. "They will be headed for the Codrex," said Gorast. "Do you think the other Toa will join them there?"

Krika glanced skyward, his twisted mouth forming a cold smile. "One can only hope, sister."

* * *

Tahu had been many things in his time as a Toa leader — decisive, arrogant, brave, contentious, noble, and almost ridiculously stubborn. One thing he had rarely been was stupid, and he didn't intend to start now.

"Wait," he said quietly to Onua. The Toa of Earth stopped digging as all three listened. They heard nothing.

"They aren't following?" wondered Gali. "Perhaps we should emerge then and head for the Codrex. From what that Matoran said, it seems to be a place of importance."

"Which is exactly why we're not going there," Tahu replied. "Onua, loop the tunnel around. We're heading back where we came from."

The Toa of Earth turned his head as best he could in the cramped space to look at Tahu. "Is that really wise?"

Tahu gave a soft laugh. "Come on, Onua — you're the one who taught me that you never go wrong doing the unexpected."

* * *

The Makuta circled the Codrex warily. The energy field around the structure was a challenge even for their powers. Only the six keystones could allow someone to pass through it unscathed. They saw no sign of the Toa Nuva, which suited Krika fine. It meant that they had succeeded in getting there before their prey.

"Take to the shadows," he ordered. Then he added, more to himself than to the others, "They are, after all, the prisons we have chosen for ourselves."

Each Makuta took up a position and waited, alone with their thoughts. Bitil banished his duplicates. He could always call them up if he needed them, but sometimes being around his past selves was annoying. They always seemed somehow naïve compared to who he was now. Actually, the mask power as a whole was more a curse than a blessing. He would suddenly find himself with injuries and no knowledge of how he had acquired them, because some future version of himself had summoned his current self into battle. It was hard to be certain how much power he could call on at any given time, since he might have expended some in a fight he didn't remember having.

He really didn't care that much about Teridax's grand Plan. Bitil's focus was on himself and his place in the Brotherhood. If he died fighting the Toa Nuva, then that would be the end of him. But if Krika or Antroz died, then perhaps he would move up, with the potential to go still further. Krika had told him once that it was a Makuta's fate to only be able to hold onto one dream — that of gaining more and more power. It was a dream Bitil embraced.

Gorast was just the opposite. Her eyes scanned the skies for the enemy, and as soon as she spotted them, they were hers to slay. It might seem odd to some that death was what she lived for, and in the end, it wasn't wholly true — death in the service of the Plan was her passion. She considered herself a Makuta of vision, just like Teridax. She could imagine what the universe would be like if the Plan succeeded . . . hear the cries of the Matoran, smell the smoke from burning villages, see armies of Rahkshi rampaging throughout the universe . . . and it pleased her no end.

As for Krika? He believed in destiny. As far as he was concerned, the Brotherhood of Makuta had sealed its fate, for good or ill, the day they decided to follow Teridax in his plan to over-throw Mata Nui. That set events in motion that nothing could stop. All he, the other Makuta, the Toa, or the Matoran could do was play their parts. He had no illusions about what the future held, regardless of whether or not the Plan suc-ceeded. *One way or the other,* he thought, *this universe is heading for a very bad end.*

From high above, Tahu Nuva eyed the three Makuta. He and his team had opted not to fly low over the swamp where they might be spot-ted, but instead to go straight up and hide in the upper reaches of the mist. Now they had circled above and behind their foes and were poised for the attack.

"Gali, you go right; Onua, left. I will target Krika," said Tahu, steel in his voice. "Hit them hard, and remember — we get one shot at this. So make it count."

Gali and Onua nodded. Then the three Toa Nuva went into power dives, screaming through the air toward a final clash with the Makuta.

INTERLUDE FOUR

Takanuva's vision of the past continues . . .

Pohatu Nuva could honestly say he had never seen anything like this "Karda Nui" place before. Of course, he hadn't seen much of anything in his short existence, but that didn't alter the fact that this place was incredible.

Karda Nui was vast, almost a world within the world. Vast stalactites hung from a ceiling that was so high, it was almost impossible to even see them without the aid of the telescopic eyepiece on Kopaka's mask. A huge, sandy plain stretched out seemingly forever — even with his Mask of Speed to help, it would have taken Pohatu a while to explore the whole place.

Pohatu turned to Lewa and pointed toward the sky. "Did you try making it all the way up yet?"

Lewa shook his head. "I need a little more practice with this Mask of Levitation first. I wouldn't want to get distracted halfway up, and then get dead, you know? Besides, our fearless leader says there's work to be done down here first."

The plain was dotted with settlements inhabited by Matoran of Light. The villagers were toiling in various places in Karda Nui, often vanishing for days only to reappear, worn out from their labors.

A flash of light in the distance drew the Toa's attention. "Uh oh," said Pohatu. "Here we go again. Grab hold!"

Lewa took hold of Pohatu's arm and let the Toa of Stone pull him along at super-speed toward the site of the sudden illumination. Onua and Tahu were already there and not faring very well. The Toa of Earth was on the ground, his chest plate scorched and still smoking, while Tahu's walls of flame were proving to be no obstacle at all.

These were what the Matoran called "avohkah," and the reason the Toa were there. At first, the villagers who labored in Karda Nui thought the place was just prone to violent lightning storms. But after more than a dozen Matoran were killed by lightning strikes, the rumor started that the bolts of energy were actually hostile and intelligent beings. The Toa's first few encounters with the avohkah seemed to verify this. The lightning bolts avoided obvious traps and seemed to go out of their way to do harm.

"Where's Gali?" asked Pohatu. "She's the only one who has been able to slow these things down."

"Off fighting another outbreak west of here with Kopaka," said Tahu, hurling fireballs to try to divert the lightning strikes. "They'll get here when they can. Meanwhile, it's up to us."

"Ah, this is the life," said Lewa, nimbly

dodging a bolt. "Wake up in the morning, have a little breakfast, and then spend all day trying to avoid being fried."

"Look at it this way," said Pohatu, as a lightning bolt shattered his hastily created rock wall. "If you don't avoid it, you won't have to worry about what to have for breakfast tomorrow. And — look out!"

A massive avohkah was headed right for where Tahu and Lewa were standing. Both Toa reacted at the same time. Lewa used his wind power to hurl a blanket of sand into the air to try to "blind" the creature, while Tahu launched a wave of super-hot fire. Neither really expected their hasty defense to work. Both braced for the painful outcome.

It turned out to be quite different from what they expected. The combination of sand and flame had resulted in a third substance, a hard, translucent, and extremely thick material that formed a wall between the two Toa and their foe. The bolt struck the wall of glass, but did not pierce it.

Lewa didn't waste time being stunned. "What are we waiting for, flame-face?"

"We work together," agreed Tahu, already adding his fire to the sand Lewa was stirring up. "And don't call me that."

"Oh, don't be such an . . . ash," Lewa replied, laughing.

When they were done, the lightning bolt was completely enclosed in a thick glass dome. It couldn't get out, and its fellow avohkah weren't having any luck freeing it. Puzzled by this, they withdrew, though no one doubted they would be attacking again soon, somewhere else.

Gali and Kopaka appeared soon after, both looking exhausted. "We drove them off," reported the Toa of Water. "But I have to remember to use water bursts, not a stream. Otherwise, um . . . ouch."

Lewa wasn't paying attention. He had spotted a spherical structure on the horizon, this one not made by the Toa. "Hey, what's that?"

Kopaka glanced at Tahu so swiftly that

none of the others noticed it. Tahu shrugged in response. "It's called the Codrex. It's . . . not important right now."

"Maybe not to you," answered the Toa of Air. "Me, I'm kind of bored with busy Matoran, angry sparklers, and sand, sand, sand. I'm going to check it out."

"No!" said Tahu, more harshly than he had intended. "You're needed here. We can explore later."

"If you don't want to come, don't come," Lewa answered, already walking away. "Don't pull all that 'big leader' stuff with me — I never voted for you."

Kopaka fired a blast of ice from his sword, completely encasing Lewa from shoulders to knees. "Tahu's team leader, and he said no. So it's no."

Later, Tahu approached Kopaka when they were out of earshot of the others. "Thanks," said the Toa of Fire. "I could have handled it, but I appreciate your support."

"Don't thank me," answered the Toa of Ice. "We should just tell them the truth about the Codrex, about all of it."

"We need to keep them focused on the avohkah, not on what comes after," Tahu argued. "There will be time enough for them to worry about that . . . all too much time, probably."

Kopaka turned away, obviously unconvinced. "It's your decision. But think about this — how would you feel if someone you trusted kept secrets from you?"

FIVE

By the time the Makuta picked up their first telepathic warning of the attack, it was too late. A fireball hurled by Tahu struck Krika in the arm, the pain making him drop his Nynrah blaster. The muddy earth opened to swallow Bitil. A sphere of water appeared around Gorast's head, catching her just after she exhaled and cutting off her air. Not in a particularly forgiving mood, Gali followed with a blast from her own weapon, catching the Makuta in an energy pincers.

Tahu wasn't going to give the Makuta time to recover. He led the Toa in another run, all three hurling whatever power they had at the enemy. Only by keeping the Makuta too off-balance to use their formidable powers did the Toa have any chance of victory.

Down below, Krika took stock of the situation and decided on a plan. He tracked Gali through the air and blasted her with shadow energy, almost knocking her out of the sky. The impact made her lose concentration and freed Gorast from the water sphere. Krika shouted at Gorast to go free Bitil from his muddy trap.

Onua broke off to pursue Gorast while Tahu zeroed in on Krika. The Makuta turned intangible, letting the Toa's fire bolts pass right through him. Incredibly, Krika was actually laughing.

"Tell me, Tahu, have you ever seen a kavinika in battle with a lohrak? It can end in one of two ways — either the lohrak kills the kavinika, or the kavinika sinks its teeth into the lohrak and slays him. What makes it amusing is that the organic tissue of a lohrak is poisonous. The instant the kavinika bites down . . . it dies."

"Is there a point to this story?" Tahu snarled, throwing his shield up just in time to blunt a blast of shadow energy.

"It's very simple," said Krika, passing unharmed through a ring of fire that had erupted around him. "Even if the kavinika wins, it loses. You might well want to keep that lesson in mind."

Not far away, Gorast was finding it rough going. Every few steps, the earth erupted, sending a half-ton of mud flying into the air. Up ahead, Bitil had managed to scramble out of the mud pit and get into the air. He had Gali on the run, or so it seemed. At the last moment, she dropped, looped around, and hurled a water blast. Bitil barely managed to evade it, but in so doing, allowed her to gain altitude. Now she was using her weapon to create obstacles made of energy in the air, forcing Bitil to fly an evasive pattern.

Still, the Makuta was not without resources of his own. Triggering his mask power, he summoned two duplicates of himself. They materialized behind Gali, swooping down and each seizing one of her arms. Together, they hurled her with tremendous force toward the swamp.

Onua spotted the flash of blue out of the corner of his eye. He whirled in midair and fired his weapon, creating a flexible platform made of energy above the swamp waters. Gali hit it hard, but it gave beneath her, lessening the damage. Onua followed it up with a hastily created land bridge linking the platform to the Codrex.

Spotting his distraction, Gorast attacked. She rocketed up from the ground and slammed into his midsection. The land bridge instantly collapsed under Gali, but she had recovered enough to stay aloft. Meanwhile, Onua grappled with Gorast, who was trying to bring her light-draining abilities to bear.

"Admit it, Toa," said Gorast. "You have always wished for a spirit as black as your armor."

"Actually, I do have a wish you could make come true," said the Toa Nuva of Earth. He reared back and struck a mighty blow, sending the Makuta spiraling downward. "A world without Makuta!"

Not far away, Tahu and Krika were locked in a duel, flame against shadow. Neither had managed to gain the upper hand. Although Tahu didn't show it, he was worried. The Toa's surprise attack hadn't been able to finish off the Makuta, and now the three of them were in for the fight of their lives.

"I would almost call this a stalemate," said Krika. "Except, of course, that you are about to surrender and beg for my mercy."

"You've been breathing too much swamp gas," Tahu replied, countering another bolt of shadow energy with a shield made of fire.

"The Codrex, Tahu," continued Krika. "Oh, we can't get in either, but Bitil is a master with energy fields. He tinkered with this one here and there. In a few minutes, it's going to implode and take the entire sphere and all its contents with it. And there will go your hope of awakening your precious Mata Nui."

Tahu had a moment of conflicting impulses. Part of him wanted to burn Krika down, while another part wondered if the Toa Nuva should surrender and hope to get a chance to undo whatever Bitil had done.

But this was not the Tahu of even a year before. He had been through too much, learned too much — most especially he had learned not to let his own nature control him. The essence of fire was action, but action without thought was like a fire that burned unchecked — it left nothing but devastation in its wake.

So, in the end, Tahu rejected both his ideas. Instead, he smiled and said, "You're bluffing, Makuta. You would no more destroy the Codrex than I would pet a Rahkshi."

"Are you so sure?" asked Krika. "Do you really want to gamble the future of your universe based on nothing but your lack of trust in others? Why would I lie about such a beautiful act of destruction?"

"If you wanted it wrecked, you had plenty of time to do that before we even got down here," Tahu answered, dodging shadow blasts as he did so. "No, there's something you want in there, or it would be gone by now. What's more, I think you want us to get it for you."

Krika chuckled. "You are just a wealth of bad theories today, Tahu. Explain that one."

"Simple. The keystone we stole from your camp — you never would have left it unprotected unless you wanted us to have it. In fact, this has all been too easy from the start. It has "Makuta trap" written all over it. And by the way, since you like the cold so much — have some on me."

Tahu hovered in midair and began rapidly absorbing all the heat from around Krika. Sensing what was about to happen, Krika tried to turn intangible again. But Tahu was faster, and Krika began to ice over halfway between his solid and ghostly state.

"Very . . . good, Tahu," Krika said, his voice sounding hollow and far away. "Too easy . . . perhaps . . . but it is about to become much more difficult. Look behind you."

"Do you really think I am going to fall for that old trick?"

"No . . . I am counting on the fact you

won't," answered Krika. "Since there really is something behind you . . ."

Against his better judgment, Tahu looked over his shoulder. Diving down toward him were Antroz, Chirox, and Vamprah, and their three shadow Matoran. All of the sudden, his team was badly outnumbered

This would *have to be the first time a Makuta has told the truth*, he said to himself. "Onua! Gali! Hunt cover!" he shouted.

It was useless, of course. Antroz's first blast of shadow energy shattered the ice forming around Krika. Vamprah flew to join Bitil, and the two closed in on Onua. Chirox hauled Gorast out of the mud, and the two circled Gali, arguing over who would make the kill. Tahu managed to land some fireballs on Antroz, but not to any great effect.

Now the six Makuta formed a V-shaped wedge in the sky and bore down on the Toa Nuva, their attacks forming a solid wall of shadow energy. Tahu, Onua, and Gali were driven back until they were pinned down near the Codrex field. One more step backward and they would hit the protective energy around the sphere and be hurled straight toward the oncoming Makuta.

"Any ideas?" Onua asked Tahu.

"Yes," said the Toa of Fire. "We take as many of them with us as we can when we go."

The Makuta hovered in midair now. "It appears your theory that we need you alive is about to be proven wrong," said Krika. "Good-bye, Tahu."

Antroz raised his arm, shadow energy swirling around his claw. Just as it was set free in a devastating burst, a sphere of super-hard ice materialized around both shadow bolt and hand. Blocked, the energy fed back into Antroz, jolting him like an angry avohkah.

"I hate good-byes, personally," said Kopaka Nuva. He had plunged out of the mists above, flanked by Pohatu and Lewa. Not far behind came the Matoran villagers Solek, Tanma, and Photok.

"Us too," said Pohatu. "In fact, we hate 'em so much we couldn't let three Makuta take off without us."

"Ever-cute idea, Antroz," chuckled Lewa. "Making your quick-retreat from above look like a planned attack on below. Did they teach you that at lying slime-sack school?"

On the ground, Tahu smiled. The Toa Nuva were still outpowered by the Makuta, but now the numbers were even. And he would take his team of Toa against any enemy, any day of the week.

"Well," he said to Onua and Gali. "Are we going to let those three show up late and have all the fun?"

"I'm for a rematch," said Onua. "How about you, sister?"

Gali bumped armored fists with her two partners. "Let's get them."

The three Toa Nuva lifted off from the ground, soaring into the final battle.

INTERLUDE FIVE

Takanuva's vision of the past continues . . .

Gali hurled a water burst at an oncoming avohkah. The creature struck the water dead-on and exploded with a bright flash of energy. Exhausted, the Toa of Water looked around, but there were no more of the sapient lightning bolts to be seen. The battle was finally over.

It had taken months, but the last of the avohkah had been defeated. Whether they might return one day was unknown, but for now, the Toa's work in Karda Nui was done. And so, apparently, was that of the Matoran of Light, who were now occupied with packing up their possessions and preparing to leave this realm.

All, that is, except one Matoran, who stood

gazing up at Gali with wide and wondering eyes.

"Can I help you?" asked Gali, smiling gently.

"What you did . . . all of you . . . that was amazing!" said the Matoran. "How can I learn to do that? How can I become a Toa?"

Gali shook her head. "I wish I could tell you . . . but I don't know myself. I'd like to think that the universe knows when it needs a hero and finds a way to bring one into being."

The Matoran pondered her words for a while. Then he brightened, "Then I will just have to make sure I am around the next time a hero is needed! That shouldn't be too hard."

The Matoran walked away, a new energy in his step. "Remember me, Toa Gali," he said over his shoulder. "You'll be hearing my name someday, whenever people talk about heroes — Takua!"

Gali laughed. She turned at the sound of others approaching and saw Tahu and the rest of the team. The Toa of Fire looked grim, even for him. "What's the matter?" she asked.

"Nothing," said Tahu, unconvincingly. "But

we need to talk . . . and I need to show you all something."

The Toa of Fire led them across the plain to the structure he had called the Codrex. A circular stone floated in empty air about five feet from the entrance. Lewa looked at it, curious, then reached up and plucked it from its invisible perch.

"Put that back!" snapped Kopaka.

"Why?" asked Lewa. "I just want to get a look at it."

The Toa of Ice started to respond, then visibly relaxed. "You know, you're right. But you'll have an easier time examining it inside the Codrex. Why don't you head on in?"

Lewa gave a nod and started forward. He had only gone about two paces when he collided with an energy field and was sent flying. When he finally crashed to earth, Kopaka was standing there. The Toa of Ice snatched the stone from him and said, "That's why." Then he marched back to the Codrex and put the stone back into the field.

The six Toa, including a chastened Lewa, approached the sphere. Tahu raised a hand and the entrance slid aside. Even Tahu and Kopaka, who knew what to expect, were surprised by what they found.

The interior was huge, dominated by machinery that none of the Toa could even begin to understand. One whole section was sealed off, and even then, the place was bigger than any the heroes had ever seen. Onua and Gali looked at complex devices with wonder, while Pohatu ran a hand along the stone wall that blocked access to the other section of the sphere.

"I could probably bring this down," he said.

"It's not our concern," Tahu replied. "This is."

The Toa of Fire tossed a fireburst toward the back wall. When it flared, the light given off illuminated six canisters standing side by side, each about nine feet high. "What are those?" asked Onua.

"They're called Toa canisters, for want of a better name," said Kopaka. "They are a means of transport. Quite remarkable, from what I have been told."

"Well . . . great," said Lewa. "It's got to be better than that dimension-hop we took to get here. So where are we going?"

There was a long moment of uncomfortable silence, with Tahu and Kopaka both waiting for the other to speak. Then the Toa of Fire said, "Nowhere."

The hatch of the Codrex slammed shut. Onua rushed to it and battered it with his enhanced strength, but it wouldn't budge. "Tahu, use your fire power — melt this thing!"

The Toa of Fire put his hand on Onua's shoulder and gently pulled him away from the hatch. "We're not leaving, brother . . . at least, not for a long time to come."

"What are you talking about?" asked Gali. "We're prisoners here?"

"Not prisoners," said Kopaka, "more like . . . emergency reserves. Remember what we were told? If Mata Nui should ever be struck down, it would be up to us to restore him to power. That is our goal and our destiny."

"Terrific," said Pohatu. "Can't we keep busy until that happens, preferably someplace other than here?"

"Try to understand," said Tahu. "Someday, the fate of the entire universe may depend on what we do. And until that day comes, it's vital that we stay together and stay whole. If we were to be killed, there would be no one to do what had to be done."

"These canisters — they will keep us safely in slumber until we are needed," said Kopaka. "When the time is right, they will be launched and will take us where we need to go. We will emerge, armed with tools and masks to carry out our mission."

Pohatu touched one of the canisters. Its top began to rotate, finally opening with a hiss. The Toa of Stone grabbed the lip of the canister, hauled himself up, and peered inside. "Right. Not so much as a carving to read in there. I don't think so."

A tremor suddenly shook the Codrex. Kopaka looked at Tahu, alarmed. "So soon? Do you think the Matoran made it out?"

"I hope so," Tahu replied. "If not . . ."

Onua read the expression in the two Toa's eyes. "Wait a moment," he said. "There's more to this than what you've told us. The avohkah were just the start, weren't they? There's worse coming."

Tahu turned away and walked to the hatch. He passed his hand over a portion of the wall and a small segment of the hatch opened. The other Toa crowded around to see what looked like a massive storm of raw energy descending on Karda Nui. Already, the Matoran structures on the plain had been incinerated. The glare was so blinding Onua had to look away, but the others could not tear their eyes away from the sight. It was overwhelming in both its majesty and sheer horror.

A vast, swirling cloud of power hovered just above the ground, extending upward for as far as the eye could see. Spears of lightning flew from it in all directions. The heat emanating from the heart of the storm fused the sand of the plain to glass in all directions.

"It's . . . incredible," breathed Gali.

"It's devastating," corrected Lewa. "And we're right in its path!"

"When it reaches full power, no living thing will be able to survive out there," said Kopaka.

Tahu shut the gap in the hatch. "The Codrex can protect the equipment inside . . . but only the canisters will protect us. So it's your choice: get into them and wait for the day we are called, or take your chances with the storm."

The Toa of Fire looked around the room. He was far from happy about the decision he was asking them to make. But he believed what Helryx had told him and Kopaka that day on Daxia. Without Mata Nui, there would be no universe, and millions, maybe billions of lives would be lost. Against that, he had to balance the freedom of six Toa. There really was no choice.

Pohatu was the first to make a move toward the canisters. "Well, I could use a nap," he grumbled as he climbed in. The lid sealed itself once he was safely inside.

One by one, Onua, Kopaka, and Gali followed suit. None looked happy, but at least they seemed to have resigned themselves to their fate. Onua paused before Tahu and said, "I can't say I agree with everything that has been done . . . but I can guess the burden you and Kopaka have been carrying. Were I in your armor, perhaps I would have done the same."

Lewa, on the other hand, was in no mood to be forgiving. "You knew this storm was coming all along," he said angrily. "And you knew we wouldn't have time to follow the Matoran out of Karda Nui. You and I are going to have a *long* talk when we wake up again, Tahu — count on it."

But there would never be any long argument between Lewa and Tahu. The special mechanism that put the six Toa to sleep in their canisters would damage their memories as well. When, 100,000 years later, they found themselves on the shore of Mata Nui, they would remember only a long and fitful sleep disturbed by dreams and nightmares. Gone would be all recollection of training on Daxia, meeting Helryx or Hydraxon, their adventures in Karda Nui, or the fate that forced them to give up millennia of their lives.

Most importantly, it had eliminated one important fact from their minds: the knowledge that, when Mata Nui awoke once more, the storm would return. And when it did, every living thing in Karda Nui would be turned to ash.

EPILOGUE

Takanuva shook his head, trying to make sense of all the images that had flashed so rapidly through his mind. One image in particular had seared itself into his consciousness — the energy storm that had torn through Karda Nui when Mata Nui awoke for the very first time.

He opened his eyes to see Helryx and Krakua standing nearby. Krakua held the krana-kraata hybrid in his hand. "Now you know," said Helryx. "We were aware the Toa Nuva would lose part of their memory in the time they spent in the Toa canisters, the better to keep our existence a secret. But we could not foresee how complete the loss would be. They are in Karda Nui now, with no idea that if they succeed in their mission, they and the Av-Matoran there will all die."

"So there's no hope? I can't believe that!" said Takanuva.

"Of course there's hope," snapped Helryx. "Why do you think we brought you here? You are a Toa of Light, try not to be quite so dim. The key to the Toa Nuva's survival can be found inside the Codrex, but they must have the knowledge you hold to be able to use it wisely. You must get to Karda Nui and warn them."

"If your organization is so powerful, why can't one of your members carry this message?"

Helryx nodded. "We have members of great power, true. But none with your ability, the mastery of Light itself. Only you can battle the Makuta on even terms . . . while we launch an attack of our own on the Makuta base at Destral."

Takanuva could guess what that meant. If the Order of Mata Nui attacked the Brotherhood, the resulting war might do what Mata Nui's death had not: wreck the universe. But he sensed there was something more to the situation and his silence showed it.

Helryx looked away and spoke again. "Recent events have led the Makuta to suspect our existence. Already one of our members, Botar, has been killed. If his mental shield was somehow breached, the enemy may be tracking our other agents even now. But one Toa, alone, might be able to make it to Karda Nui."

There was no choice, of course. If this was all some kind of trick, Takanuva had no doubt he had the power to make this Helryx pay. And if it wasn't . . . the lives of the six beings he admired most were in grave danger.

"I'll go," said the Toa of Light. "But what about the Toa Mahri? Will someone be here to help them defend the city in my absence?"

"Oh," said Helryx, smiling, "I don't think that will be a problem."

Takanuva turned to see an armored titan enter the room, dragging another along behind him. He was tall and strong, but looked as if he had been through a war. Both his armor and mask were damaged. But that wasn't what struck Takanuva as most strange. Rather, it was the complex breathing apparatus he wore — could this being not breathe air?

"Meet Brutaka," Helryx continued, "an Order of Mata Nui member with a somewhat less than sterling record . . . still, desperate times. The Mahri may need a little convincing to work with him . . . but I can be very persuasive."

"And this is Dweller," Brutaka said, kicking his white-armored captive across the floor. "A Dark Hunter planted here long ago to keep an eye on the city — and to kill you, Toa. He has a way of getting into your head . . . but I decided to be nice and let him keep his own."

"Wait a minute, I've heard of you from the Mahri," said Takanuva. "You betrayed your oath and almost killed two teams of Toa. It took your own partner to put you down." He turned to Helryx. "This is your idea of help for Metru Nui?"

Helryx's expression turned dark. "Understand something, Takanuva. We are in a war. Maybe we have been since the day the Brotherhood struck down Mata Nui. And in a war, you don't always get to choose your allies or test them first to make sure they are good and pure enough. I would recruit Dark Hunters and Pit prisoners if I thought it would bring the Makuta down."

"And what kind of universe would that leave you with?" asked Takanuva.

"One full of beings still free to make their own mistakes," answered Brutaka.

Takanuva said nothing, simply looked from Brutaka to Helryx, unsure of which one he disliked more in that moment.

Krakua finally spoke up, trying to break the tension. "Brutaka will be your means of transport to Karda Nui, using the dimensional travel power of his mask. It's faster than going by Toa canister, if a little more dangerous."

Takanuva looked again at Brutaka's mask. There were hairline cracks in a number of places. It was amazing it was still functioning at all. But there was no turning back now.

"I'd have to be insane to trust him," said the Toa of Light.

"Haven't you figured it out yet?" said Helryx, offering her hand. "You have to be insane to be a Toa at all. It's the first requirement for the job."

After a long moment, Takanuva reached out and shook her hand. Maybe she was right, he conceded. Maybe in a time of crisis, the old rules don't apply — and maybe being a hero was a lot more complicated than he thought.

"Take this," said Krakua. The object he offered Takanuva was, of all things, a sundial. "You may need it."

Takanuva took it even as Brutaka triggered the power of his mask. A hole opened in space, its edges ragged and distorted, and its size fluctuating wildly. Taking a deep breath, Takanuva plunged into it, to begin the strangest journey of his life.

"Do you think he'll make it?" asked Krakua as the hole disappeared with an audible pop.

"He has to," answered Helryx. "If I am right, the Makuta have much bigger plans than just controlling Karda Nui — and we may need the Toa Nuva, if we hope to stop them. He has to get them out of the core before the energy storm consumes them all."

"Should we have told him the rest?" Krakua said, obviously a little uncomfortable with what had and had not been shared.

"About what is going to happen to him? And what his true destiny may be?" Helryx gave a bitter laugh. "No, Krakua. If we are wrong, then it would all be for nothing. And if we are right . . . the truth might well drive him mad."

Helryx, Brutaka and Krakua left the chamber then, to begin the long walk from the Archives to the surface of Metru Nui. Each knew what was about to happen: an all-out conflict between the forces of the Order of Mata Nui and the Brotherhood of Makuta.

They walked slowly towards the light high above, sure in the knowledge that what they were about to do would change the universe forever . . . or destroy it.